P9-DNL-622

SECRET AGENTS
JACK & MAX STALWART

THE ADVENTURE
IN THE AMAZON:
BRAZIL

BOOKS BY ELIZABETH SINGER HUNT

THE SECRET AGENT
JACK STALWART SERIES

BOOKS BY ELIZABETH SINGER HUNT

THE SECRET AGENTS
JACK AND MAX STALWART SERIES

Book 1–The Battle for the Emerald Buddha **(Thailand)**

Book 2–The Adventure in the Amazon **(Brazil)**

Also:
The Secret Agent Training Manual:
How to Make and Break Top Secret Messages

And:
Swamp Mysteries: The Treasure of Jean Lafitte

For more information visit
www.elizabethsingerhunt.com

THE ADVENTURE IN THE AMAZON:
BRAZIL

Elizabeth Singer Hunt
Illustrated by Brian Williamson

WEINSTEIN
BOOKS

PH CASS COUNTY PUBLIC LIBRARY
400 E. MECHANIC
HARRISONVILLE, MO 64701

0 0022 0570405 5

Copyright © 2017 by Elizabeth Singer Hunt

Illustrations copyright © 2017 by Brian Williamson

All rights reserved. No part of this book may be used or reproduced in any manner whatsoever without the written permission of the Publisher. For information address Weinstein Books, 1290 Avenue of the Americas, New York, NY 10104.

Printed in the United States of America.

Cataloging-in-Publication data for this book is available from the Library of Congress.

ISBN: 978-1-60286-361-3 (print)
ISBN: 978-1-60286-362-0 (e-book)

Published by Weinstein Books
A member of Hachette Book Group
www.weinsteinbooks.com

Weinstein Books are available at special discounts for bulk purchases in the U.S. by corporations, institutions and other organizations. For more information, please contact the Special Markets Department at Perseus Books, 2300 Chestnut Street, Suite 200, Philadelphia, PA 19103, call (800) 810-4145, ext. 5000, or e-mail special.markets@perseusbooks.com.

First edition

LSC-C

10 9 8 7 6 5 4 3 2 1

For Secret Agent Theo

GLOBAL PROTECTION FORCE ALERT

THE WORLD'S MOST PRECIOUS TREASURES ARE UNDER ATTACK!

Secret Agents Courage and Wisdom recently thwarted an attempt to steal the *Emerald Buddha* from the Grand Palace in Thailand. The GPF believes that the mastermind behind this crime was also behind the thefts of Picasso's *Acrobat* painting and a Fabergé egg from Russia. If this is true, we have a madman on our hands.

All agents must be prepared to travel at a moment's notice. Anyone witnessing someone or something suspicious should report it immediately to Gerald Barter, the Director of the GPF.

THINGS YOU'LL FIND IN EVERY BOOK

Global Protection Force (GPF): The GPF is a worldwide force of junior secret agents whose aim is to protect the world's people, places, and possessions. It was started in 1947 by a man named Ronald Barter, who wanted to stop criminals from harming things that mattered in the world. When Ronald died, under mysterious circumstances, his son Gerald took over. The GPF's main offices are located somewhere in the Arctic Circle.

Watch Phone: The GPF's Watch Phone is worn by GPF agents around their wrists. It can make and receive phone calls, send and receive messages, play videos, unlock the Secret Agent Book Bag, and track an agent's whereabouts. The Watch Phone also carries the GPF's Melting Ink Pen. Just push the button to the left of the screen to eject this lifesaving gadget.

Secret Agent Book Bag: The GPF's Secret Agent Book Bag is licensed only to GPF agents. Inside are hi-tech gadgets necessary to foil bad guys and escape certain death. To unlock and lock, all an agent has to do is place his or her thumb on the zipper. The automatic thumbprint reader will identify him or her as the owner.

GPF Tablet: The GPF Tablet is a tablet computer used by GPF agents at home. On it, agents can access the GPF secure website, send encrypted e-mails, use the agent directory, and download mission-critical data.

Whizzy: Whizzy is Jack's magical miniature globe. Almost every night at 7:30 p.m., the GPF uses him to send Jack the location of his next mission. Jack's parents don't know that Whizzy is anything but an ordinary globe. Jack's brother, Max, has a similar buddy on his bedside table named "Zoom."

The Magic Map: The Magic Map is a world map that hangs on every GPF agent's wall. Recently, it was upgraded from wood to a hi-tech, unbreakable glass. Once an agent places the country shape in the right spot, the map lights up and transports him or her to their mission. The agent returns precisely one minute after he or she left.

THE WORLD

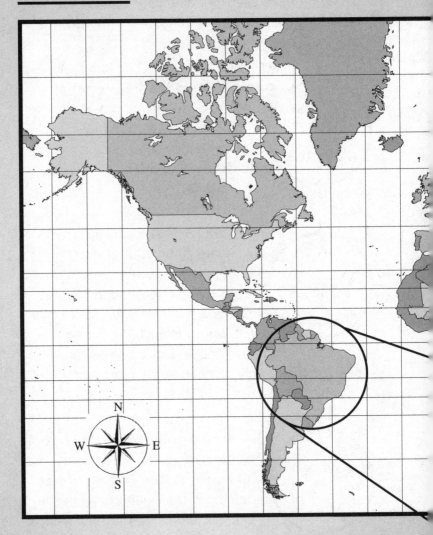

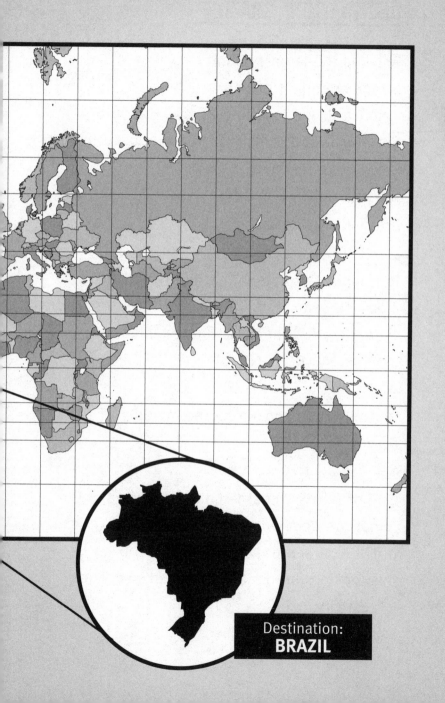

Destination:
BRAZIL

DESTINATION: BRAZIL

Brazil is the largest country on the continent of South America. It got its name from the Brazilwood, a type of tree that used to grow along its coast.

Brasília is its capital city.

Portuguese explorers first discovered the area 500 years ago. They ruled Brazil from 1500–1815 A.D. In 1822, Brazil gained its independence.

Portuguese is spoken by the majority of Brazilians.

One of Brazil's most famous landmarks, *Christ the Redeemer*, is an enormous statue of Jesus. It stands on a mountain top overlooking Rio de Janeiro, Brazil's second-largest city.

THE AMAZON RAIN FOREST: FACTS AND FIGURES

A "rain forest" is a dense jungle that gets a lot of rain.

About 60 percent of the Amazon rain forest is located in Brazil. The Amazon is home to the largest collection of plants and animals in the world.

More than 16,000 species of trees, 1,300 species of birds, 40,000 species of plants, and 2.5 million species of insects call the Amazon rain forest home.

There are fears that 40 percent of the Amazon rain forest will be gone by 2025.

Some of the world's deadliest predators live in the Amazon, including flesh-eating piranhas, poison dart frogs, venomous snakes, and jaguars.

Threats to the Amazon rain forest include logging, ranching, drilling for oil, and mining. Mining for gold is especially harmful because the mercury used to extract it can get into the water supply, poisoning living things.

THE AMAZON RAIN FOREST: INTERESTING INHABITANTS

The **piranha** is a fish with razor-sharp teeth and an aggressive appetite for meat. It lives in the Amazon basin and in the lakes around Brazil.

Poison dart frogs are small, brightly colored frogs that secrete a deadly neurotoxin through their skin. Neurotoxins can affect the nervous system, leading to potential death.

The **emerald tree boa** is a nonvenomous snake that squeezes its prey to death. The snake eats small mammals, birds, and frogs, and can grow 6 feet (1.8 meters) long.

Pitcher plants are carnivorous plants that lure insects inside. Once the bug falls to the bottom of its cavity, it's dissolved and digested.

The **capybara** is the largest rodent in the world. The heaviest Brazilian capybara ever recorded weighed 200 pounds (or 91 kilograms)! Capybaras are a favorite food of caimans and jaguars.

The **scarlet macaw** is one of several kinds of macaws in South America. They are known for their scarlet red feathers. In the wild, they can live up to fifty years.

SECRET AGENT PHRASEBOOK FOR BRAZIL

THE STALWART FAMILY

Jack Stalwart: Nine-year-old Jack Stalwart used to work as a secret agent for the Global Protection Force, or GPF. Jack originally joined the GPF to find and rescue his brother, Max, who'd disappeared on one of his missions. Jack tracked Max to Egypt, where he saved him *and* King Tut's diadem, or crown. After that, Jack and Max retired from the force. The brothers live with their parents in England.

Max Stalwart: Twelve-year-old Max used to be a GPF agent too. He was recruited after filling out a questionnaire online, and pledging his young life to protect "that which cannot protect itself." Max's specialty within the GPF is cryptography, which is the ability to write and crack coded messages. Recently, Max narrowly escaped death in Egypt, while protecting King Tut's diadem. After Egypt, he and his brother, Jack, decided to take a break from the GPF.

John Stalwart: John Stalwart is the patriarch of the family. He's an aerospace engineer, who recently headed up the Mars Mission Program. For many months, the GPF had fooled John and his wife, Corinne, into thinking that their oldest son, Max, was at a boarding school in Switzerland. Really, Max was on a top secret mission in Egypt. When that mission ended, Max's "boarding school" closed, and he returned home for good. John is an American and his wife, Corinne, is British, which makes Jack and Max a bit of both.

Corinne Stalwart: Corinne Stalwart is the family matriarch. She's kind, loving, and fair. She's also totally unaware (as is her husband) that her two sons used to be agents for the Global Protection Force. In her spare time, Corinne volunteers at the boys' school, and studies Asian art.

GPF GADGET INSTRUCTION MANUAL

Secret Language Decoder: When you need to translate a language that you don't understand, use the GPF's Secret Language Decoder. First, set this rectangular device to your primary language. Then, decide how you want to use it. Choose "listen" to eavesdrop or "read" to scan and translate text. Translations will appear on the screen. The Secret Language Decoder is a must-have for all foreign missions.

Virtual Teleporter (VT): The GPF's VT is a handheld device that receives and transmits live 3-D images. It looks like a square makeup compact with two halves that hinge open. One half is the camera; the other is the receiver. Perfect for sending and receiving images while in remote areas. The VT works without a wireless signal.

The Grapple: With the GPF's Grapple, no one will know you're about to snap up a crook instead of a photo. That's because the Grapple is disguised to look like an old-fashioned camera. Just point the lens at your target and push the black button. A sticky, strong string will fly out of the lens, attaching itself to the crook. To reel him or her in, hook the Grapple on to something strong and push the red button. It can carry up to a 450-pound man.

Chapter 1
The Bee

Jack Stalwart was a nervous wreck. And it wasn't because he was on a mission for the Global Protection Force, or GPF. He was standing onstage in the gym at his school, participating in the annual geography bee. The geography bee was a student competition to see who knew more about the world's geography. The final three contestants were Benjamin O'Dell, Cynthia McNulty, and nine-year-old

Jack Stalwart. "Now we're advancing to the knockout round," said Ms. Paulson, the moderator of the bee. She was one of Jack's teachers. Ms. Paulson was sitting at a table in front of the stage and reading from a piece of paper.

Jack was nervous. One wrong answer and he'd be dismissed.

Jack knew what it felt like to be asked to leave the stage. In last year's spelling bee, he was knocked out when he misspelled the word "reconnaissance." It was particularly embarrassing because he should have known how to spell *that* word. Reconnaissance was the art of gathering information on enemy forces, which is exactly what Jack did almost every night for the GPF.

The first question went to twelve-year-old Benjamin. Benjamin was one of the smarter kids at school. He was wearing a plaid shirt and tan pants.

"In what country would you find the temple of Angkor Wat?" asked Ms. Paulson.

"Easy," thought Jack. Thanks to his recent mission in Southeast Asia, he knew that answer. Unfortunately, Benjamin knew it too.

"Cambodia," said Benjamin smugly.

Ms. Paulson nodded. "Correct," she said.

"Jack," said Ms. Paulson, reading from her paper. "What is the capital city of Finland?"

"Helsinki," said Jack, without missing a beat.

"Correct," said Ms. Paulson.

Jack ran his fingers through his brown hair and sighed in relief. Ms. Paulson directed the next question to eleven-year-old Cynthia McNulty.

"In what country would you find the world's tallest mountain, if measured from the seafloor?" she asked.

Cynthia was quick to answer. "Nepal," she said proudly.

"I'm sorry," said Ms. Paulson. "The correct answer is the United States of America."

"Huh?" said Cynthia with a puzzled look on her face.

Jack was confused too. Everyone knew that Mt. Everest was the tallest mountain

on earth. Jack could testify to that. After all, he'd nearly climbed to the top when he was chasing a bunch of thieves who were after a yeti skull in Nepal.

Ms. Paulson explained. "Mt. Everest is the tallest mountain, if measured from the mountain's base," she said. "But Mauna Kea is the tallest, if measured from the seabed. Mauna Kea is on the island of Hawaii, which is in the United States of America."

Cynthia walked off the stage, her head hung low. Her ponytail swayed back and forth as she walked.

"That means we
have our final two!"
said Ms. Paulson.
"Jack Stalwart and
Benjamin O'Dell!"

The audience
erupted with
applause. Jack could
hear his parents and
his older brother,
Max, cheering him
on. Max gave Jack an
encouraging thumbs-up. Jack
was happy to see Max in the audience.
They were like best friends.

"Come on, Jack!" said his dad.

"You can do it, sweetie!" said his
mum.

As soon as the applause died down,
Ms. Paulson got back to business. "The
first person to miss a question is

eliminated," she said, "leaving the remaining student as the winner."

The butterflies in Jack's stomach were fluttering now.

"Benjamin," said Ms. Paulson. "What country is the birthplace of opera?"

"Italy," said Benjamin.

"Drat," thought Jack. That was an easy question.

"Correct," said Ms. Paulson. Then, she turned to Jack.

"In 1979, the Serra Pelada gold mine was established in northern Brazil," she said. "What is the name of the state where the gold mine was located?"

The audience gasped. This was the most difficult question yet! It was extremely specific and, unlike the other questions, required some knowledge of history.

Or did it?

Jack wondered whether he could reason through to an answer. He wasn't alive in 1979, and hadn't heard of the Serra Pelada gold mine. In fact, he didn't even know that there was gold in Brazil. But Ms. Paulson had said something about a northern state. Jack knew that Brazil was divided into 26 states (and one federal district). Only a handful were in the north. Two of the biggest states were Amazonas and Pará. Since they covered most of the north, Jack reckoned if he guessed one of them, he'd have a nearly 50/50 chance of being right. The trick was guessing the right one.

Jack took a deep breath and hoped for the best. "Amazonas," he said.

Ms. Paulson's face dropped. Jack knew what she was going to say before she even said it.

"I'm sorry," she said. "That's incorrect. The correct answer is Pará."

The last thing Jack remembered was Ms. Paulson telling him to leave the stage. Jack was in a dazed state. He walked off like a zombie.

"Let's give a round of applause to our new geography bee winner," said Ms. Paulson. "Benjamin O'Dell!" Ms. Paulson presented Benjamin with a trophy. On top of the trophy was a globe.

The audience erupted with cheers.

"And let's not forget our second-place finisher, Jack Stalwart!" said Ms. Paulson.

The audience clapped for Jack too, but by that point Jack was too numb to care. He walked from the stage to his parents and brother.

"We're so proud of you!" said his father.

"*I* didn't even make it into the semifinals," said Max, giving Jack a playful punch in the arm.

"Give me a hug, sweetie," said his mother, throwing her arms around him. "You're such a clever boy!"

"I don't feel very clever," said Jack.

"People are only as clever as the question they're given," said his dad. "No one in the audience knew that answer including us, and we're not stupid."

"I guess so," said Jack.

"How about we get an ice cream?" said his mother.

Ice cream always made everything feel better.

As Jack walked toward the door, he turned to see Benjamin kissing the trophy like a tennis player who'd just won Wimbledon. After seeing that, Jack vowed never to lose the geography bee again. If that meant he had to study every atlas, geography book, and map he could get his hands on, he'd do it. In the meantime, there was ice cream.

"Let's get out of here," said Jack, pushing the doors open. Then, the Stalwarts left the gym.

Chapter 2
The Not-So-Funny Joke

When they got home, Max and Jack
looked at the clock in the Family Room.
It was 7:15 p.m.

Max stretched out his arms and faked
a yawn. He winked at Jack. "I'm beat
from tonight's excitement," he said.
"Plus, I have some homework to do. I'm
going to my room."

"Yeah, me too," said Jack, following
his brother's lead. "Mrs. Carney gave us

two sheets of math."

The boys' father, John Stalwart, beamed with pride. "Every night at 7:30 p.m., the two of you are upstairs doing your homework. It's enough to make a father proud."

Little did their dad know, Jack and Max weren't just doing their homework. They were secret agents for the Global

Protection Force, or GPF. Nearly every night at 7:30 p.m., Jack and Max were sent on missions to protect the world's most precious people, places, and possessions.

Jack and Max raced up the steps, nodded to each other, and then opened their bedroom doors.

As soon as Jack entered his room, he walked over to Whizzy, the miniature globe on his bedside table. Whizzy wasn't just an ordinary globe. He was the vehicle through which the GPF announced the location of Jack's next mission.

He did it by coughing up a virtual jigsaw piece in the shape of a country. The piece hung in the air until Jack grabbed it with his fingers and swiped it over to the Magic Map. Once Jack placed it over the right country, the Magic Map came to life. It turned into a portal that transported Jack to the location of his next mission.

Realizing that it was thanks to Whizzy that he did so well in the geography bee, Jack patted Whizzy on the head. "Thanks, pal," he said.

Just then, Whizzy woke up and began to spin. After gathering enough speed, Whizzy coughed up a country shape. It hung in the air for a few seconds before Jack realized what it was. When he did, he started to laugh. He quickly swiped it over to the Map. After putting it in the right spot, the name "Brazil" lit up and then disappeared.

Jack raced to his bed and pulled out his Secret Agent Book Bag from

underneath. He placed his thumb on the zipper and unlocked the bag. He looked inside. A new gadget had been added to the GPF's bag of tricks—the VT, or Virtual Teleporter.

Jack put his thumb on the zipper again, this time to lock it. After strapping the Book Bag over his shoulders, he stood in front of the Magic Map. A light began to grow from inside the country of Brazil. Eventually, it filled his entire room.

"Off to Brazil!" he said, telling the map he was ready to go.

Within seconds, the light flickered and burst, sucking Jack into the Magic Map.

The last thing Jack remembered before leaving his room was the muffled sound of his brother, Max, next door saying something too.

Chapter 3
The Surprise Attack

When Jack arrived, he found himself in the middle of a dense, dark forest. The leaves on the trees above him blocked the sunlight above. The air was hot and humid, and beads of water were forming on his face. He lifted his arm and wiped his brow with his sleeve. A drop of water fell from a leaf above and landed on the tip of Jack's nose.

SQUAWK!

Jack jumped.
SQUAWK!

Jack steadied himself and looked in the direction of the sound. A pair of scarlet macaws was perched on a nearby branch. Jack was relieved. Scarlet macaws were harmless. But the large green snake coiled on the opposite branch wasn't. It was the emerald tree boa—a snake that could squeeze its prey to death. Jack took a few steps back. Although it wasn't venomous, he didn't want to become the snake's next meal.

Marching in a line at the base of another tree was a string of bullet ants. The bullet ant was known as the "world's most painful insect." Its sting felt like the agony of being shot by a bullet. Jack looked down at his GPF standard-issue pants and boots and said a silent "thank you" to Mr. Richardson.

Mr. Richardson was the GPF's tech guru. He'd recently developed an insect repellent called "Get off my clothes!" It was ten times better than anything on the market. All secret agent's clothes and boots had been sprayed with it.

Given the macaws, bullet ants, and emerald tree boa, there was no doubt in Jack's mind that he was in the Brazilian rain forest. He couldn't have been more excited. Ever since reading about the adventures of the American president Teddy Roosevelt, Jack had wanted to visit.

In 1914, Mr. Roosevelt and a team of explorers had successfully navigated an unexplored river of the Amazon. In his honor, the river was later named the Roosevelt. Roosevelt's adventure was filled with danger, death, and disease. Jack didn't want to encounter those things on his mission. But he was secretly hoping for an adventure like Roosevelt's.

BLAM!

Out of nowhere, Jack was hit from behind. Whatever it was had knocked him to the ground. Jack quickly rolled over and stood up. He put his hands out. After all, it could have been a *Panthera onca*, or a Brazilian jaguar. Jack had to be prepared for another strike.

As soon as Jack saw what had hit him, he barreled forward and shoved it to the ground. He playfully rubbed its face into the mud. It was Jack's brother, Max.

"Let go!" shouted Max, in a muffled voice.

"Not until you apologize for knocking me down," said Jack.

"I couldn't help it," said Max. "I landed a bit funny."

Max was taller and stronger than Jack. He quickly twisted his body around, grabbed Jack's arms, and pinned *him* to the ground.

"Give up?" asked Max, yanking gently on Jack's arm.

"Okay! Okay!" said Jack.

Max released Jack, and wiped the mud off of his face. Jack sat up and rubbed his sore arm.

"We're in the rain forest," said Jack.

"You don't say," said Max teasingly. It was pretty obvious where they were.

Jack gave his brother an annoyed look.

Something in their Secret Agent Book Bags started to vibrate. They opened their bags to find the VT lighting up.

The VT was one of the newest GPF

gadgets. It could project a live, 3-D image anywhere in the world. Unlike cell phones, it didn't require a wireless signal, which was great in remote places like the Amazon jungle. Max took it out and opened the case. He put the receiving end on the ground.

A small image of Harry Billingsby sprang up from the bottom half of the

VT. Harry worked for the GPF and was Director Barter's right-hand man. He was wearing thick-rimmed glasses, a gray

suit, and a red-and-blue striped tie.

"Hello, Courage and Wisdom," said Harry, using Jack and Max's code names.

"Hi, Harry," said the boys in unison.

Harry cleared his throat. He quickly got to business.

"As you know," Harry began, "many people think that the rain forest holds the key to helping and curing human disease."

Jack and Max nodded. They'd recently read a GPF report on that. Chemicals from rain forest plants had already been used to treat stress, muscle aches, and diarrhea. It was just a matter of time before scientists found cures for other more serious things like cancer.

"That's why we sent our lead botanist, Ginny Rosebottom, to the area," explained Harry. "She was to photograph, catalog, and research new plants."

"And?" asked Max, wondering what the problem was.

"Ginny's disappeared," said Harry, looking concerned.

"What happened to her?" asked Jack, leaning in.

"We don't know," said Harry, tweaking his glasses a bit. "That's what we need the two of you to find out."

"When was she last seen?" asked Max.

"Yesterday morning," said Harry. "She participated in a video call. Since then, no one's been able to reach her. And she didn't show up for today's call."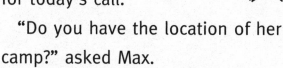

"Do you have the location of her camp?" asked Max.

"I've sent the directions to your Watch Phones," said Harry.

"We'll start there," said Jack.

"Don't worry," said Max, trying to reassure Harry. "We'll find Ginny."

"I hope so," said Harry. Then, his image disappeared.

Chapter 4
The Dangerous Jungle

Max closed the VT and returned it to his
Book Bag. Jack looked at the screen on
his Watch Phone. The directions to
Ginny's camp had come through.

"I've got the information from Harry,"
said Jack.

He tapped his Watch Phone twice. A
forested map of the area appeared on
the screen. There was a blue dot
representing their current location, and a

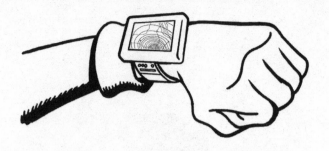

red dot signifying Ginny's camp. A squiggly yellow line showed the best route in between. Standing on top of the blue dot was a tiny white person, which would represent Jack and Max's journey.

According to the map, it was going to take five miles or two hours for the brothers to get there. They looked to the path ahead. There were fallen trees and crooked branches in their way. The ground was wet and muddy. The walk was going to be tough, not to mention confusing. The forest looked the same from every direction.

Jack took the GPF's Jungle Marker out of his book bag. The fluorescent orange marker was specially designed to stick to tree bark. Jack marked the tree to his right with an orange "X" on both sides.

"In case our Watch Phones stop working," said Jack with a smile.

"I'll take the lead," said Max, only half listening to Jack. "You watch from behind."

The boys set off. Almost immediately, Max spied something yellow on the ground ahead. He swung his arm out to stop Jack from going any farther. Max's voice deepened to a more serious tone.

"Poison dart frog," said Max.

Jack peered over Max's shoulder. Sure enough, there was a tiny yellow-and-black frog perched on a log. He was cute, but deadly. Jack recognized it from his book, *The World's Most Deadly Species*. The toxin secreted through its skin could kill several grown men.

Max and Jack stayed clear of the frog and walked around it. Jack continued to mark every fifth tree with an orange "X." After two hours, they arrived at a clearing. Jack looked to the map on his Watch Phone. The tiny person was now standing on top of the red dot.

"This is it," said Jack.

Max spied something ahead. "That looks like a GPF Jungle Hut," he said, pointing to an extremely large, tented structure.

Jack recognized it too. The GPF's Jungle Hut was made of a waterproof,

tearproof, and bulletproof fabric. It kept
the occupant safe and the inside
temperature cool—ideal conditions for
the hot and dangerous Brazilian rain
forest.

The first thing the boys did was to
survey the tent. They walked around the
perimeter, looking for signs of trouble.
But there was nothing unusual about the

outside. Jack tried to open the door. It was locked.

"This calls for the Magic Key Maker," said Jack, taking the gadget out of his book bag.

The GPF's Magic Key Maker was a clever device that could mold itself to any keyhole and instantly form a key. Jack slid his inside the lock. He turned the Key Maker to the right and the door opened.

As soon as Jack and Max entered, they were surprised. Ginny's hut didn't look disturbed. In fact, it looked as though she was still there. The CD player was playing soothing classical music, and there was a half-drunk cup of tea sitting on the wooden desk.

"Ginny?" called Max, expecting her to respond. But there was no answer.

Jack walked over to her desk and looked more carefully at the tea. The milk in the drink was starting to curdle. He touched the cup. It was cold.

"The tea isn't fresh," said Jack. "It was made a while ago."

Jack and Max searched the other rooms, but couldn't find any clues. When they returned to the main room, something on Ginny's desk caught Jack's eye.

It was her journal. It was sitting next to a photo of Ginny holding a rare orchid. Next to that was a gold paperweight on top of a stack of papers. Jack opened the book to the last entry.

"It's from yesterday," said Jack, recognizing the date.

Wednesday, June 21
Walked farther north today, along the river. Came across a man-made bridge. Planning to explore more tomorrow. Could lead me to an undiscovered tribe.

The fact that Ginny mentioned an "undiscovered tribe" was worrying. Not all of the indigenous people of the Amazon were friendly. Some used spears and poison blow darts. If Ginny had run

into one of them, there was no telling
what had happened to her. Jack and Max
had to hurry. Time was running out.

Chapter 5
The Pits

Max tapped the screen on his Watch Phone and expanded the map. Seven miles northeast was a river.

"That might be where the bridge is located," said Max. "If we find it, we might find Ginny."

The boys left the clearing and stepped back into the jungle. A piglike animal called a tapir sprinted across their path. Overhead, Jack heard a group of howler monkeys growling like a bunch of bears.

Since the river was seven miles northeast, Jack and Max had two choices. They could trudge north through the forest and then take a right toward the river. Or, they could head for the river first and then walk along its banks. At some point, they'd hopefully come across the bridge.

Jack and Max decided to take the second option. There was more sunlight near the river. After hiking for a while, they heard the sound of running water.

"It's the river," said Max. "We're getting close."

Before they knew it, Jack and Max were at the river's edge. Dangerous-looking rapids were flowing by. Rapids are fast-flowing sections of a river that crash over the boulders in its way.

Steering clear of the river, the boys walked along the bank. Jack continued to mark every fifth tree, while Max used his Watch Phone to chart their path.

"We should be there any minute," said Max as they approached the seven-mile mark.

Sure enough, they found what they were looking for—a rope bridge crossing the river. It was ten feet above the water. When they got to it, they looked for Ginny or evidence that she'd been there. But there was nothing.

"I wonder if she crossed over," said Max.

"Let's find out," said Jack.

Jack and Max surveyed the bridge. There were wooden planks for steps and ropes for handrails. Jack and Max tugged on the ropes and walked on a couple of planks. When they were satisfied it

would hold their weight, they carefully
crossed.

As soon as they got to the other side,
they noticed something peculiar. There
were plastic garbage bags stacked along
the bank, and a dugout boat tied to a
post. A path led from the bridge to the
forest. At the edge of the forest, there
were ten donkeys with burlap bags and
pickaxes hanging from their saddles.

"What's that all about?" asked Jack.

Max shrugged his shoulders.

The boys followed the path. As soon as they passed under the trees, they found themselves in an enormous clearing. In the dusty, barren earth there was a collection of large pits or holes dug into the earth.

Scrambling over the holes was a bunch of dirty, sweaty men. Jack and Max counted ten of them, which easily equaled the number of pits in the ground. From what the brothers could tell, they looked Brazilian. They also looked like they'd been working in the sun for years. Their skin was dark brown and wrinkled like a raisin.

Jack and Max watched as one of the men was lowered into a pit. A few minutes later, a bucket of dirt was sent up, and another man poured the contents

of the bucket into a sieve. After the finer dust and debris fell through the holes of the strainer, a single nugget of earth was left. It was passed to a third man who cleaned it. The object was washed thoroughly and given to a fourth man who studied it through a magnifying glass. The man's lips curled in disgust as he threw the rock to the ground and walked off.

"They're digging for gold," said Max.

Just then, a threatening voice rang out.

Jack and Max pulled out their Google Goggles. The GPF's Google Goggles were high-powered binoculars that could magnify objects two miles away. Jack and Max placed the devices over their eyes.

They focused in on the source of the sound. An older man was walking toward the miners. He was wrinkled from the sun like the others, but he carried himself differently. He held himself like a boss.

There was a green bandanna around his neck, and a dirty cigarette hanging off of his bottom lip. On the top of his upper lip was a bushy mustache. A rug of curly gray chest hair popped out from the top of his half-unbuttoned shirt. Hooked on to his belt was a holster with an antique pistol in it.

The man began to shout at his men. It sounded like he was speaking Portuguese, which neither Jack nor Max understood. Jack pulled out his Secret Language Decoder. The GPF's Secret

Language Decoder was a rectangular device that could translate a foreign language into English on the screen. Jack turned the Decoder on. The boys read the translation as the man talked.

"We're moving out tomorrow!" he barked. "This is the last day to find gold. Anyone finding a nugget will get double rations. Anyone NOT finding gold will get nothing. For some of you, that's three days without food. If you're hungry, I suggest you work harder!"

The man pulled the pistol out of his holster, and shot it into the air.

BANG!

The men jumped. So did Jack and Max.

Terrified, the men quickly went back to work.

"I think I know what happened to Ginny," said Jack.

"Me too," said Max. "I think she found these guys. And I think they found her too."

Chapter 6
The Boss Man's Office

Max switched his Google Goggles to
optimum length, and his vision shot
through the air. He scanned the sides of
the camp and spotted ten hammocks
hanging from trees. Scattered near the
base of the hammocks were bags and
pots for cooking. He reckoned this was
where the men slept and ate. At the
back of the clearing, there was an
outhouse or toilet. Next to that was an

even bigger shack. It was this one that the boss man was walking toward.

"I think I found his office," said Max.

Max switched the setting on his Google Goggles to "X-ray." His vision moved through the wooden walls of the shack and into the inside. There was a desk, a bed made of wood, and two chairs. One of them was empty. The other had a person sitting in it. When Max saw who it was, he gasped.

"It's Ginny!" said Max.

Jack recognized Ginny from the picture on her desk. Ginny didn't look hurt, but her wrists and ankles were tied to the chair.

"That explains why Ginny didn't return to the hut," said Jack.

Just then, the boss man entered the shack. He sat in the chair opposite Ginny.

"We need to hear what he's saying," said Jack.

The brothers put their goggles away, and scurried as quietly as they could alongside the clearing. At the back of the hut was a cutout for a window with a mosquito screen on it. They ducked down underneath and switched on their Secret Language Decoder. This time, however, they didn't need it. Surprisingly, the man spoke English.

"You won't get away with this," said Ginny. She lifted her chin proudly to show that she wasn't afraid.

The man laughed.

"People call me Pistol Pedro," he said, "not only for my pistol-sharp intellect but also because of my friend here."

Pistol Pedro gently tapped the pistol that was in his holster.

"For decades, I have moved through the Amazon rain forest like a shadow," said Pedro. "I've been stealing gold since Serra Pelada, never getting caught."

Jack and Max looked at each other. They'd heard the name Serra Pelada before. It was the name of the mine in Jack's geography bee question. Jack wondered if the GPF had weaseled that question into the competition to better prepare him for his next mission.

Pedro took a long drag from his
cigarette and then put it in an ash tray
on his desk. Pistol Pedro pulled some
sunflower seeds out of his pocket, and
put several into his mouth.

"I work for a very powerful
organization," said Ginny confidently.
"After they rescue me, they will come
after you."

Pedro chewed his seeds for a bit, then spit the shells on the floor. "Hah!" he said. "They won't rescue you." He leaned into Ginny. "They won't even *find* you."

Ginny's confidence started to crack.

"I was thinking that you might enjoy a scenic boat ride," said Pedro. "One that will take you down river."

When Ginny remembered what was downstream, her face went white. "I'll never survive the rapids," she said, pleading for the man to reconsider.

"That's the plan." Pedro sneered. Then, he opened the door and left.

Chapter 7
The Wrong Call

If Jack and Max were going to rescue
Ginny, they had to do it quickly. They
crept around the corner of the hut and
studied the clearing. From what they
could tell, most of Pedro's men were still
working in the pits. A few of them were
walking with Pedro toward the river.

As soon as the coast was clear, Jack
and Max opened the door of the shack
and dashed inside. It was obvious from

their Watch Phones and book bags that they worked for the GPF. When Ginny saw them, she sighed with relief.

"Thank goodness you're here!" she said excitedly. "I thought I was going to find a long-lost tribe. Instead, I found these *thugs*!"

Max lifted his left boot, and opened the heel. Inside was a pocketknife. He took it out, opened it, and began to cut the ropes from Ginny's wrists. Jack was trying to look out for Pedro and his men, but there weren't any windows at the front of the office.

Ginny carried on. "As soon as I saw them," she said, "I knew what they were up to. But they grabbed me before I could cross back over the bridge."

Max managed to cut the last thread of the rope that tied Ginny's wrists.

"Thank you," she said, rubbing her sore wrists.

"There's nothing to worry about now," said Max, putting his pocketknife back in his boot.

BLAM!

The door to the office flew open.

Pistol Pedro was standing in the doorway, flanked by three of his men.

"My men told me they saw a couple of kids go into my office," he said. "But I didn't believe them."

Pedro took the cigarette out of his mouth and threw it to the ground. He stamped on it with his leather boot and crushed it into the floor.

"It looks like they were telling the truth," he said.

Pedro leaned into Jack and Max.

"Nobody comes into my office without my permission," he growled. Then, he nodded to his men.

Before Jack and Max could act, the men from behind Pedro rushed in. They ripped the book bags off of their backs and flung them into the corner. Tossing Jack, Max, and Ginny to the floor, they quickly tied their wrists together. Jack and Max tried to wriggle free, but it was no use.

"These must be the friends you were talking about," said Pedro to Ginny. "I told you they'd be no match for me. The good news is that you won't be lonely on that river trip."

Jack looked at his Book Bag, which was in the corner of the shack. If only he could reach it. He could use any of a number of gadgets inside to catch these goons. But it was too far out of his way.

Just then, Jack had another thought. If he could move his fingers just so, he might be able to tap a few commands on his Watch Phone. From there, he could send an emergency call to the GPF, and Pistol Pedro and his men would be history.

But unfortunately for Jack, he wasn't the only one thinking about his Watch Phone. Pedro noticed the gadget peeking out from under the ropes on Jack's wrist. He leaned down and yanked the Watch Phone off of his arm.

"Ouch!" yelled Jack. He didn't want to seem like a wimp, but that really hurt.

"It isn't gold," said Pedro, holding the silver-colored device up to the light, "but it will fetch a good price."

Pedro stole Max's Watch Phone too. Pedro put both gadgets in his pocket. Jack and Max's hopes for escape powered down at the same time as their Watch Phones.

Pistol Pedro signaled to his men. They dragged Jack, Max, and Ginny away from the shack, and toward the river. When they arrived at the river's edge, the men tossed Jack, Max, and Ginny to the ground.

THUMP!

Next to them was the dugout boat that the boys had spied when they crossed the bridge. Normally when people rode rapids, they didn't use heavy log boats. They rode them in inflatable rafts or light kayaks, so that they had a better chance of navigating the rapids and the rocks.

Unfortunately for Jack, Max, and Ginny, the boat that Pedro had planned for them was anything but light. In fact, it looked like the kind of boat that Roosevelt used when he explored the Amazon one hundred years ago.

The men hauled Jack, Max, and Ginny into the boat. A shadow came over them, blocking the sunlight from their eyes. Pistol Pedro leaned over them and untied the boat from the wooden post.

"Have a nice trip," he grumbled.

Then with one swift push, Pistol Pedro plunged the boat into the water.

Chapter 8
The Roaring Rapids

The rushing rapids swiftly carried Jack,
Max, and Ginny away from the camp.
Despite its weight, the log boat didn't
sink. Instead, it barreled over the rocks,
knocking the wooden bottom underneath
and causing Jack's, Max's, and Ginny's
teeth to chatter. Jack looked back at
Pistol Pedro and his men. They were
walking back to the clearing. Pistol
Pedro checked the burlap bags that were

tied to the donkeys, then disappeared under the trees.

"We have to stop him before he leaves!" said Jack, almost shouting over the roaring sound of the river.

"I'll get us out of these ropes," said Max. "You calculate the distance."

Jack knew what Max was talking about. Without the help of their Watch Phones, they needed a way to mark the start and end point of their journey, as well as the distances in between.

Jack used the bridge as their start point, and began to count trees on the eastern side of the river. But the boat was moving too fast. There was no way that Jack could count that quickly.

Then, he remembered the orange marks he'd left on the trees. Many of them were along the river bank. Jack shifted his focus to the other side. Sure enough, he spotted one of his orange "X"s. As long as he could see an "X," he knew they were within five miles of the bridge and between five and seven miles from Ginny's camp.

Max had already figured a way out of the ropes. Even though his wrists were tied, he could maneuver his hands and fingers. He opened the left heel on his boot for the second time that day and grabbed his pocketknife. He turned around and handed it to Ginny.

"Can you hold this vertically?" he asked.

Ginny nodded. She held the knife as steadily as she could. But it wasn't easy. The boat was bobbing up and down in the rapids.

Max carefully moved the rope around his wrists up and down against the knife. After twenty swipes, the rope fell off of Max's wrists and to the floor of the boat.

Grabbing the knife from Ginny, he cut the ropes from her wrists too. But before he could free Jack, the boat slammed into a rock. The back end lifted up, and Jack fell out of the boat. He landed headfirst into the raging rapids.

Chapter 9
The Devil's Falls

Panicked, Max leaned out over the side of the boat.

"Jack!" shouted Max.

There was no sign of Jack. He'd completely disappeared.

"Where did he go?" screamed Ginny.

"I don't know!" said Max, desperately searching for his brother.

For several long seconds, there was no sign of Jack. Then, Ginny spied something.

"Over there!" she shouted, pointing to something bobbing in the water behind them.

Jack's head broke the surface. Jack gave Max a thumbs-up. But Jack wasn't doing well. He'd hit his head on a rock, and it was hurting badly.

Unfortunately, Jack didn't have time to think about his head. If he didn't get back in the boat, he might lose Max and Ginny all together.

He swam frantically, but couldn't catch the boat. It was moving faster than his body was floating. Plus, Jack's legs and feet were dangling underneath him and scraping against the rocks below. It was slowing him down. He lifted his legs upward, and tried to ride the rapids on his back.

Ahead of the boat, he could see a hanging vine. He got an idea.

"Max!" yelled Jack as he pointed to the vine ahead.

When Max saw it, he knew what Jack wanted them to do. Max turned to Ginny.

"We need to grab a hold of it," said Max. "It's our only chance to save Jack."

Max and Ginny seized the vine as soon they were under it. They sat down so that their bodies could help anchor the boat. If they could keep the boat steady for a few more seconds, there was a chance that Jack would be thrust upon them. But the rapids were extremely powerful. The vine was starting to slip from their hands.

"Hurry!" shouted Max to Jack, his face red with effort.

"We can't hold on much longer!" shouted Ginny.

Jack tried to position his body just right.

WHAM!

Jack hit the front of the boat straight on. He grabbed on to it with his tied wrists and let the force of the rapids slide his hands along the top edge. With all the strength he could muster, he lifted his feet and his legs up, and over the side.

SNAP!

The vine broke. The boat was catapulted back into the rapids again.

But Jack was safe. He lay at the bottom of the boat, sopping wet and totally exhausted. Max and Ginny collapsed too; their arm muscles shaking. Ginny noticed something on Jack's head. She reached out to touch his forehead. When she pulled back, Jack noticed what looked like red paint on her fingers.

"You've cut yourself," said Ginny. "We need to get back to my hut so that I can put some oils on it."

Max was definitely worried about his brother's head. But he was more concerned with getting their boat off of the river.

Jack looked to the bank and caught a glimpse of another orange mark. They were still within miles of Pistol Pedro's and Ginny's camps. But how were they going to get off of the river? Pedro made sure they didn't have an oar. Plus, there was a worrying roaring sound ahead. A fine mist was spraying up above the rapids.

"What's that?" asked Max.

"It's Devil's Falls," said Ginny, looking as though she'd just remembered. "It drops two hundred feet before crashing to the rocks below."

Jack and Max looked at each other. They couldn't survive a plunge like that. Not with a boat as heavy as this one. Jack tried to think of a way out. But the stress of it all was preventing him from thinking clearly. The mist from the fall was getting closer. So too was the crashing sound.

"We can't just sit here," said Ginny, panicked. "We have to do something."

Jack looked at the trees. He couldn't see any more orange marks, which meant they were now more than five miles from the bridge. The noise of the falls was deafening. They would soon be on the edge of them. Ginny was right. They needed to do something—and fast.

To the right of the fall, Jack spied something. There was a series of large boulders that formed a wide upside-down U. Since the boulders were off to

the side, they created a pool-like area
where the water spun around in an eddy.
From there, there was a series of
boulders that led to the bank.

As soon as Jack saw it, he had an idea.

If they could
navigate their
bodies into that
eddy, they might
have a chance.
The only way to
do that,
however, was to
risk their lives.
They had to
jump into the
deadly rapids.

Chapter 10
The Only Way Out

Jack showed Max and Ginny the pool of water. "We need to jump out as far as possible," said Jack.

Max and Ginny agreed with the plan.

"On the count of three?" said Max.

"One . . . ," shouted Max.

Jack, Max, and Ginny stood up.

"Two . . . ," he yelled.

They lifted one of their feet onto the side of the boat.

"Three . . . ," he hollered.

And they hurled their bodies into the water.

Jack, Max, and Ginny crashed into the frothing river. As soon as they surfaced, they swam as hard as they could toward the bank. Fortunately for them, the currents swiftly took them into the safety of the eddy.

Within seconds, their boat sailed off the edge of the river and disappeared from view. The next thing they heard was the horrible sound of it splintering on the rocks below.

Chapter 11
The Brazilian
Peppertree Plant

Jack, Max, and Ginny looked at one
another with a mix of horror and relief.
They clambered over the large boulders
and toward the riverbank. When they
reached land, they collapsed.

In the distance, they heard the sharp
whistle of an agouti, a large rodent that
lived in the forest. A troop of army ants
marched on the ground nearby.

Since Jack had recently seen the last of the orange marks, it meant they were a mile or two south of Ginny's camp. The trio decided to follow the river north until they came to the first "X." From there, they could cut westward and follow the remaining signs.

When they found Ginny's camp again, they were more than relieved.

"Help yourself to whatever you need," said Ginny as she opened the door to her hut.

Max grabbed some purple acai berries from a nearby fruit bowl.

Jack pulled a bottle of water out of Ginny's fridge. But instead of drinking it, he put the cool plastic object on his aching head.

"I have something for that," said Ginny, making her way to her desk.

She opened one of the drawers and

pulled out a vial. After uncorking it, she poured a few drops of oil onto her finger and rubbed it on Jack's cut forehead.

"What *is* this stuff?" asked Jack, already feeling better.

"This is from the Brazilian peppertree plant," said Ginny. "It's great for killing bacteria and soothing cuts. This is one of the plants I've been studying."

With Jack on the mend, Max's focus shifted to Pedro. The outlaw had said

something about "moving out." If Jack
and Max were going to nab him, they
had to act fast. Max scribbled something
on a piece of paper from Ginny's desk.

"Can you get this message to Harry
Billingsby?" asked Max.

"Sure," said Ginny. Then she read what
was on the paper. "Are you mad? You
can't go after Pedro on your own!"

"Don't worry about us," said Max.
"We've got a plan."

Jack shot a look at Max. He didn't
know anything about a plan.

Max plucked a gold-colored
paperweight from Ginny's desk. "Do you
mind if we take this?" said Max.

"Sure," said Ginny, confused by the
request. "You can have it."

Jack sensed that Max was ready to
leave. "Thanks again for taking care of
my head," said Jack.

"It's the least I can do," said Ginny, smiling. "You two saved my life."

"Be safe," said Max. "Good luck with your research."

"Thanks," said Ginny. "I'll make sure to send your message to Harry."

Jack and Max said their last good-byes and left Ginny's hut.

Chapter 12
The Rope Bridge

As soon as they stepped outside, Jack turned to Max. "So what's the plan?"

Max told him what he was thinking. Jack shook his head in concern.

"I don't like it," said Jack. "Too risky."

"Trust me," said Max. "He's greedy enough to fall for it."

Jack reluctantly agreed to go along with Max's scheme. They followed Jack's orange marks toward the river again and

headed north along the bank. After
several miles, they arrived at the bridge.

Part one of Max's plan was to lure
Pedro and his men from the clearing and
toward the river. But from the looks of it,
they were already there. Pedro and the
miners were tying up their belongings to
their donkeys.

"Looks like they're heading out," said
Jack.

"Time to move to part two," said Max.

Jack ripped a long strip of fabric from
the bottom of his shirt, and tied one end
to his left wrist. He let the other end
hang down.

While Jack was preparing himself, Max
used his knife to partially cut through
the railing on the southern side of the
bridge. Max tugged on it to make sure
that it wouldn't completely give way.
When he was satisfied it wouldn't, he

gave Jack the thumbs-up.

Jack stepped onto the rickety bridge, keeping his left hand on the upper rope railing. He carefully balanced his weight on the planks, one step at a time. When he reached the middle of the bridge, he called out to Pedro.

"Hey, you!" he shouted.

Pedro turned around, stunned in silence at the sight of Jack. After all, he'd sent Jack, Max, and Ginny to an almost certain death. Since part of Max's plan was to annoy Pedro, Jack decided to lay it on thick.

"Yeah, you, you raisin!" said Jack. "You might be able to earn a little cash by selling that chest hair of yours. Someone might want to turn it into a rug!"

Pedro scowled. "Why you—" he said, making his way toward the bridge.

Jack continued to toy with Pedro. He

lifted the large, shiny gold nugget in his right hand into the sky.

"Missing something?" taunted Jack.

Pedro's eyes opened wide in shock. Then they turned black with anger.

"That's one of my nuggets!" he said with a scowl. "Nobody steals from me and gets away with it!"

Pedro marched toward Jack and the bridge. Pedro's men followed behind their boss.

"I'm going to give you one last chance," said Pedro, seething. "Give me that nugget!"

As soon as Pedro stepped on the bridge, it sloped to his left. While the miners noticed the bridge's weakness, Pedro was too consumed with anger to feel it. Pedro continued to march toward Jack. His men, however, stayed behind.

"If you want it," said Jack, "you'll have to come and get it!"

Pedro put his hand on his holster, and took out his pistol. He walked toward the middle of the bridge. Jack grabbed the railing with his left hand and casually tied the hanging end of the fabric around his wrist to the railing.

Max burst from behind the wooden post and quickly sliced through what was left of the rope railing on the southern side. That half of the railing

collapsed, sending Pedro sailing toward the rapids below.

"Ahhh!" he wailed as he fell.

On his way down, Pedro grabbed a hold of one of the hanging planks. In doing so, he accidentally let go of his beloved pistol. It fell into the river with a "plunk."

"My baby!" he yelled.

Pedro had more things to worry about than his gun. With the lower half of his body dangling in the river, the currents were threatening to sweep him away.

"Somebody help me!" he shouted.

But Pedro's men didn't want to help him. Pedro had treated them badly for years. Instead, they ran for the donkeys. They opened the burlap bags, and stuffed as many gold nuggets as they could into their pockets. Then, they retreated into the forest and disappeared.

Chapter 13
The Big Catch

Jack, on the other hand, was in a much more fortunate position. He'd prepared himself for the fall. All he had to do was to lift himself upward, step onto the top edge of a plank, untie his wrist, and then shimmy across to the other side of the river. Once he did, he hopped off the bridge and gave Max a high five.

"Told you it would work," said Max.

"Good call," said Jack. "He *was* greedy enough."

Jack opened his right hand. In it was the gold "nugget." "Do you think Ginny wants her paperweight back?" asked Jack.

Max and Jack laughed at the joke.

Just then, they heard a familiar sound from above. It was the sound of a helicopter arriving. And not just any helicopter. It was a GPF helicopter.

"Looks like our message got through," said Max.

At Ginny's Jungle Hut, Max had scribbled the following:

TO: harrybillingsby@gpfhq.com

SUBJECT: Urgent Message for Harry Billingsby

Ginny is safe, but we need help apprehending her captor, Pistol Pedro.

He's 60 years old and wearing a green bandana. Pedro has a hairy chest and leathery skin.

Send a helicopter ASAP to the rope bridge 7 miles northeast of Ginny's hut.

Thanks.

Secret Agents Courage and Wisdom

The helicopter hovered overhead and a door slid open. A man in a dark suit and dark sunglasses lifted a six-inch-long (15.2 cm) silver tube to his eyes. He was looking through it at the ground. Jack and Max recognized it immediately. It was the GPF's "Identity Scanner," an excellent gadget for recognizing criminals in a crowded place.

The device worked by comparing the physical features of a suspect against thousands of arrest photos. If there was a match, the inside of the tube turned green and the name of the bad guy appeared on the outside. If there was no match, the inside of the tube turned red.

Since Pistol Pedro had never been caught before, his description wasn't in the GPF's records. That's why Max told Harry in the message what Pedro looked like.

The man in the suit zeroed in on Pedro's hairy chest. Once he'd been identified, the man pulled out his "Grapple."

The GPF's Grapple looked like an old-fashioned camera. There was a lens at the front and two buttons at the top, one red and one black. But instead of snapping up photos, the Grapple snapped up criminals. It did this by sending out a sticky, strong string from inside the fake lens.

As soon as the man had Pedro in his sights, he pushed the black button. The string flew out and stuck itself around Pedro. The agent hooked the Grapple to a metal bar inside the chopper, and clicked the red button. The gadget began to reel Pedro in.

"Let go of me, you alien!" hollered Pedro as he tried to shake off the string. "I have information. If you let me go, I'll tell you what I know!"

Jack and Max laughed. All they needed to know was that Pedro was a crook. Pedro was now sixty feet in the air, too far away for Jack and Max to hear him.

"Someone tried to hire me," he shouted. "I received a coded text—"

The door shut before Pedro could finish his sentence. Then the chopper lifted off and disappeared over the forest.

Chapter 14
The River Revealed

Jack and Max were happy to see the end of Pedro.

"Nice work," said Max, giving Jack a fist bump.

"What should we do about the miners?" asked Jack. After all, the men who worked for Pedro had scampered off into the jungle with a lot of gold.

"The Brazilian authorities can take care of them," suggested Max.

Just then, Jack remembered something.

"We should have asked for a ride!" said Jack.

Without their gadgets, they had no way of getting home.

"Do you think our stuff is still in the shack?" asked Max.

"It's worth a shot," said Jack.

Jack and Max carefully shimmied across the bridge. When they got to the other side, they dashed through the forest and into the clearing. Ahead was Pedro's office. They headed for it.

Throwing open the door, they looked inside.

Pedro had cleared everything out, except for two GPF book bags in the corner. Jack and Max were relieved.

"I guess they were useless without our thumbprints," said Jack.

The boys unlocked their bags, and

took out their Portable Maps. The GPF's
Portable Map was a smaller version of
their Magic Map from home. It could
transport them wherever they needed to
go. They laid them on the floor, and set
their destination to England.

After a small light inside the country
grew, they shouted "Off to England!"

They next thing Jack knew, he was in
his bedroom at home. The clock on his
bedside table said 7:31 p.m.

Chapter 15
The Adventurer

Jack looked around. Max wasn't there.
He knocked three times on the wall that
separated his room from his brother's.
From the other side, three knocks came
back. Jack breathed a sigh of relief. Max
had returned safely too.

Jack grabbed the GPF Tablet from his
bedside table and logged into the GPF
secure site.

GPF NEWSFLASH

After evading law enforcement for more than thirty years, the notorious outlaw, Pistol Pedro, was finally apprehended in Brazil. GPF Agents Courage and Wisdom worked together in his capture. The Brazilian government has expressed its thanks. Pedro is currently being question by both GPF and Brazilian authorities. A search team is now looking for Pedro's associates who escaped into the jungle.

In related news, Amazon rain forest scientist Ginny Rosebottom has been found and is back to work. She is continuing to research the healing effects of the Brazilian Peppertree leaf, among other newly discovered rain forest plants. She's expected to publish her findings within weeks.

Jack smiled to himself. He opened another tab. After inputting the GPS coordinates of Ginny's camp, he waited for the topographical map of the area to show up. He wanted to see the name of the river that he and Max had traveled on.

Jack traced the route they'd taken from Ginny's camp to the river. When he saw the name of the river, his jaw dropped open. It was none other than the Roosevelt—the same river that Teddy Roosevelt had navigated down one hundred years earlier! Although Jack had only traveled down a small portion of it, he felt like a true explorer. Jack logged out.

He walked over to his bookcase and pulled the world atlas off the shelf. Jack carried it to his bed and sat down. Next year, *he* wanted to be the one kissing that geography bee trophy. If it meant that he had to study a page every night for the next 364 nights, he'd do it. With that in mind, Jack cracked open his book and started reading.